AF228471

INSIDE MLS

PHILADELPHIA UNION

BY THOMAS CAROTHERS

abdobooks.com

Published by Abdo Publishing, a division of ABDO, PO Box 398166, Minneapolis, Minnesota 55439. Copyright © 2022 by Abdo Consulting Group, Inc. International copyrights reserved in all countries. No part of this book may be reproduced in any form without written permission from the publisher. SportsZone™ is a trademark and logo of Abdo Publishing.

Printed in the United States of America, North Mankato, Minnesota
052021
092021

Cover Photo: Gregory Fisher/Icon Sportswire/AP Images
Interior Photos: Michael Perez/AP Images, 4–5, 9; Graham Hughes/The Canadian Press/AP Images, 6; Drew Hallowell/Getty Images Sport/Getty Images, 10, 42; Chris Gardner/Getty Images Sport/Getty Images, 12; John Iacono/Sports Illustrated/Set Number: X17938 TK1 R6 F19/Getty Images, 15; John G. Zimmerman/Sports Illustrated/Set Number: X17936 TK2 R6 F5/Getty Images, 16–17; Dave Tennenbaum/AP Images, 19; Brian Garfinkel/Getty Images Sport/Getty Images, 21; Matt Rourke/AP Images, 23; Matt Slocum/AP Images, 24–25, 35, 37; Don Ryan/AP Images, 26; Gavin Baker/Icon Sportswire/AP Images, 29; Noah K. Murray/AP Images, 30; Gregory Fisher/Icon Sportswire/AP Images, 32; Barbara Johnston/AP Images, 39

Editor: Patrick Donnelly
Series Designer: Dan Peluso

Library of Congress Control Number: 2019954320

Publisher's Cataloging-in-Publication Data

Names: Carothers, Thomas, author.
Title: Philadelphia Union / by Thomas Carothers
Description: Minneapolis, Minnesota : Abdo Publishing, 2022 | Series: Inside MLS |
    Includes online resources and index.
Identifiers: ISBN 9781532192609 (lib. bdg.) | ISBN 9781098210502 (ebook)
Subjects: LCSH: Philadelphia Union (Soccer team)--Juvenile literature. | Soccer teams--
    Juvenile literature. | Professional sports franchises--Juvenile literature. | Sports
    Teams--Juvenile literature.
Classification: DDC 796.334--dc23

TABLE OF CONTENTS

FIRST
PLAYOFF PUSH

Most expansion teams have to wait several years to make the playoffs. In the case of the Philadelphia Union, it took just two seasons.

Being a brand-new team presents unique challenges. The players have never competed together. Often they are players other clubs didn't want. And the team has to figure out lots of new challenges on the fly, such as how to replace injured players.

The Union faced all of these obstacles upon joining Major League Soccer (MLS) in 2010. They lost half of their 30 games and won only eight. However, the next year was a different story.

Goalkeeper Faryd Mondragón was a big part of the Union's success in 2011.

Brian Carroll, *right*, played strong midfield defense for the Union.

With a year of experience, the team began coming together. The additions of goalkeeper Faryd Mondragón, center back Carlos Valdés, and defensive midfielder Brian Carroll proved key, too. That trio helped the Union cut their goals allowed from 49 in 2010 to just 36 in 2011. Through the 2019 season, that remained the fewest in team history. The improved defense didn't lead to many more wins. The Union still won just 11 of 34 games in 2011. But they rocketed into playoff contention on the strength of 15 draws.

The final draw came with a playoff berth on the line. Understanding the importance of the game, a team-record crowd of 19,178 fans packed the Union's home stadium in Chester, Pennsylvania. The team and its fans were eager for a historic day. But they were also hoping to avoid disaster against lowly Toronto FC.

As the 2011 regular season was nearing a close, the Union found themselves standing in the middle of a seesaw. There were six Eastern Conference teams in the hunt for just five playoff spots, and Philadelphia was right in the middle of that pack. Only a few points separated the teams. A Union win in the second-to-last game of the regular season would not only clinch a playoff spot. It would vault the team into first place in the conference.

However, a loss to Toronto could put the Union in danger of falling behind their rivals in the tightly packed Eastern chase. It turned out that Philadelphia got something right in the middle.

LE TOUX COMES THROUGH

The sunny day saw a bright outlook for the Union. Star forward Sébastien Le Toux took advantage of a Toronto defensive lapse to open the scoring just before halftime. Le Toux's strike, assisted by midfielder Justin Mapp, sent the home fans into the break buzzing about the Union's playoff hopes.

Le Toux was Philadelphia's leading goal-scorer with 11 on the season. The Frenchman had done his part to help his team in its playoff push. His goal against Toronto was his 10th in the Union's previous 11 games.

However, despite already being eliminated from the playoffs, Toronto would not quit. Just 12 minutes into the second half, the visitors quieted the home crowd with a tying goal.

If the score held, Philadelphia would claim one point in the standings instead of three. With so few points separating first place and a possible conference title from sixth place and

Sébastien Le Toux, *left*, battles with Toronto FC's Ty Harden.

missing the playoffs entirely, the Union wanted more. Their fans were anxious as the second half ticked away.

In the end, neither team could take the lead. As the final whistle sounded, draw No. 15 was good enough

Union coach Piotr Nowak waves to the crowd after the draw with Toronto FC.

for Philadelphia. It meant the Union were headed to the playoffs for the first time in team history.

Fans dressed in the team's blue and gold. They sang and danced, playing horns and drums, to celebrate their team's achievement. Union head coach Piotr Nowak and goalkeeper Mondragón thanked the fans and told them to get ready for the upcoming playoffs.

QUICK OUT

The regular season wasn't quite over. Philadelphia's draw against Toronto continued a team-record eight-game unbeaten streak. That run came to an end five days later in the season finale. The Union lost 1–0 on the road against the New York Red Bulls. Philadelphia fell to third place after Houston won its final game to finish one point ahead of the Union.

That set up a matchup between Houston and Philadelphia in the conference semifinals. The Dynamo were an experienced team just a few years removed from winning back-to-back MLS Cups. The Union were making their playoff debut. The results turned out to be about what one might expect.

Philadelphia's Justin Mapp (22) tries to hold off Adam Moffat of the Houston Dynamo during the 2011 MLS playoffs.

Philadelphia hosted the first game on October 30. Houston's André Hainault scored in the sixth minute. Le Toux countered a minute later. The first playoff goal in Union history tied the match 1–1. However, the Dynamo regained the lead before halftime and held on for a 2–1 victory.

When the series shifted to Houston on November 3, the Union needed to win to stay alive. That didn't happen. The Dynamo's Brian Ching scored just before halftime, and the Union's season ended with a 1–0 loss. Houston, in its sixth MLS season, went on to its third MLS Cup in 2011, losing 1–0 to the Los Angeles Galaxy.

The Union had exceeded expectations in their second season. But they would soon find that maintaining that success was easier said than done.

A RICH
HISTORY

While Philadelphia has only been represented in MLS since 2010, the city has a long history with soccer. Years earlier, Philadelphia had two different teams in the North American Soccer League (NASL). Long before that, Philadelphians cheered on a successful squad from the nearby town of Bethlehem. The tradition of those teams helped pave the way for the birth of the Union.

STARTING WITH STEEL

A century before the Union first hit the field, Philadelphians were thrilled by the success of Bethlehem Steel. The team played in an industrial town about 60 miles (97 km) north of Philadelphia.

Philadelphia Atoms goalkeeper Bob Rigby makes a save in the 1973 NASL playoff final.

The team was formed in 1907 by workers from the
Bethlehem Steel mill. Over the next 23 years, the Steel became
one of the most successful teams of the early days of soccer in
the United States. The Steel won several league championships
and a number of tournament cups. During their run of success,
they won six American Cups, including four in a row from 1916

Chris Dunleavy (5) of the Atoms challenges the Dallas defense during the 1973 NASL playoff final.

to 1919. The American Cup, now known as the US Open Cup, is the oldest ongoing national soccer tournament in the country.

But soccer's popularity began to fade in the United States. The Steel folded in 1930, and it would be a long time before pro soccer returned to eastern Pennsylvania.

BACK FOR MORE

More than 40 years after the Steel played their last game, professional soccer was back on the rise. The hairstyles were longer, the shorts were shorter, and many teams played on Astroturf instead of grass. However, top-level soccer had returned to Philadelphia. The NASL admitted the Philadelphia Atoms as an expansion team in 1973.

Much like MLS today, the NASL was the top level of competition in the country. The league operated from 1968 until 1984. At times it featured some of the top players from around the world, along with big, enthusiastic crowds. It did not take long for Atoms fans to celebrate a championship. In fact, it took only a matter of a few months.

The Atoms played in Veterans Stadium, home of the Eagles and Phillies, the city's pro football and baseball teams, respectively. They lost just two of their 19 games in their inaugural season. The Atoms finished the year by beating the Dallas Tornado 2–0 in the NASL playoff final. Local fans weren't used to this level of success. At the time, Philadelphia had celebrated just two professional championships in any sport since the 1940s. In recent years, the Eagles and Phillies had been especially bad.

Philadelphia Fury goalkeeper Keith MacRae, *bottom*, grimaces as he makes a save against the New England Tea Men in a 1978 NASL match.

The Atoms were hailed for their quick success. But the team fell on hard times just as quickly. By 1976 the Atoms had folded.

Two years later, the NASL returned to Philadelphia as the Fury were born. The team had a rock n' roll flair—literally.

TAKING IT INDOORS

In the 1970s and 1980s, some soccer fans fell in love with an indoor version of the game. It was played on a hockey rink covered with artificial turf instead of ice. The Philadelphia Fever were one of the founding members of the Major Indoor Soccer League (MISL). The Fever played in the famed Spectrum, home of Philadelphia's pro hockey and basketball teams. However, the Fever never saw the kind of popularity those other sporting events did. By 1982 the Fever were gone. Ten years later, so was the MISL.

Several popular musicians of the era, including Peter Frampton and Paul Simon, were part of the 15-person ownership group.

The Fury were one of six teams to enter the league in 1978. Like the Atoms, the Fury's best season was their first. Unlike the Atoms, that best season amounted to a 12–18 record and a first-round playoff exit. The Fury lasted just three seasons. After averaging fewer than 5,000 fans in the 56,000-seat Veterans Stadium in 1979 and 1980, the team moved to Montreal. Philadelphia would be left without top-level professional soccer for another 30 years.

SONS OF BEN

Just over 26 years after the Fury played its final game, the Sons of Ben came into being in 2007. The name was a nod to Benjamin Franklin. The famous US Founding Father spent much

The Sons of Ben supporters' group is older than the team itself.

of his life in Philadelphia. The Sons of Ben originally formed to support the idea of bringing an MLS team to Philadelphia.

Many members of the group originally cheered for DC United, which played 140 miles (225 km) away. However, members of the group wanted a team to call their own.

The group quickly grew from a few members to a few thousand. This happened around the same time MLS was beginning its rapid growth. The league was looking for cities that would enthusiastically support a new team. The Sons of Ben represented exactly that. In 2008, just a year after the Sons of Ben were founded, the supporters got the news. The league announced that Philadelphia would enter MLS as its 16th team.

FOUNDING THE UNION

A little over a year after MLS announced Philadelphia was getting a team, that team got its identity. Fans were asked to vote on the team's name. And on May 11, 2009, they found out the team would be called the Union. The name was a reference to the union of America's original 13 colonies. Philadelphia was that union's first capital.

The team paid homage to the original colonies and their fight for independence from Great Britain with more than just its name. The Union chose the primary colors of navy blue and gold to honor the Continental Army's uniforms during the Revolutionary War. The team's logo features 13 stars to represent the original colonies. A rattlesnake in the middle of the logo recalls one of the symbols of the revolution.

Team owner Jay Sugarman, *left*, and Philadelphia mayor Michael Nutter unveil the Union's logo outside City Hall in Philadelphia on May 11, 2009.

Less than a year after the Union was given its identity, the team played its first game. A century after Bethlehem Steel dominated the field, Philadelphia was officially back in big league soccer.

CHAPTER 3

MELTING POT

The city of Philadelphia is distinctly American, a hub of business, politics, and history that also served as the nation's first capital. Yet "the City of Brotherly Love," as Philadelphia is known, has embraced soccer players from around the world wearing the Union's blue and gold uniforms.

Despite being born in France, Sébastien Le Toux is practically considered a native Philadelphian for what he meant to the Union. The striker was the first player signed by the Seattle Sounders as they became an MLS team in 2009. However, he made his name in American soccer for what he did in two separate stints with Philadelphia.

A hardworking attacker with a no-nonsense attitude, Le Toux was selected by Philadelphia in the 2009 MLS

High-scoring forward Sébastien Le Toux was one of the Union's first stars.

Freddy Adu, *right*, wrapped up his MLS career in Philadelphia.

Expansion Draft. He quickly worked his way into the hearts of Union fans by scoring a hat trick in the team's first home game in 2010.

Le Toux scored 25 goals in his first two seasons with Philadelphia before a trade sent him to Vancouver for the 2012 season. But he wasn't gone for very long. After spending 2012 in Vancouver and then with the Red Bulls in New York, he was back in Philadelphia before the next season began.

Le Toux celebrated his return by scoring a goal in the 2013 season opener. He scored 24 more over the next four seasons to finish his time in Philadelphia with 50 goals. He was traded to Colorado near the end of the 2016 season, and he played just one more year. As the decade ended, his 50 goals were the team's all-time best. He was also the leader in games played (175) and assists (50) over the Union's first 10 years.

"They traded me once, they traded me twice, but now I'm here forever, and nobody can trade me from that," Le Toux said in 2018, when he became the first player to be inducted

FREDDY ADU

Forward Freddy Adu was meant to be the next big thing. DC United drafted Adu in 2004 when he was just 14 years old. On April 3 of that year, he became the youngest player in MLS history. Two weeks later he became the youngest to score a goal. Unfortunately, Adu's career did not pan out as many hoped. Philadelphia was his last MLS stop. He played for the Union from 2011 to 2013, scoring seven goals in 35 games.

into the Union's Ring of Honor. "It's awesome. I'm a part of this team and this club and I can't be more proud of that."

MORE EUROPEANS

Tranquillo Barnetta was born in St. Gallen, Switzerland. The creative midfielder/wingback spent most of his career in Europe. But he helped direct the Philadelphia attack in 2015 and 2016. A versatile player up front for the Union, Barnetta helped Philadelphia end a string of four straight seasons without a playoff appearance in 2016.

In a three-year stint away from his native France, Vincent Nogueira was the midfield engine for the Union in the mid-2010s. One of the best passers in team history, Nogueira played for Philadelphia from 2014 to 2016. Like Barnetta, he was instrumental to the Union's run to the 2016 playoffs.

BORN IN THE USA

It just wouldn't feel right if the team representing the original capital of the colonies didn't have a bit of American flavor. The Union have featured a number of homegrown players in their fight to become a top team in MLS.

Alejandro Bedoya was born just a couple hours away from Philadelphia in Englewood, New Jersey. He joined the Union

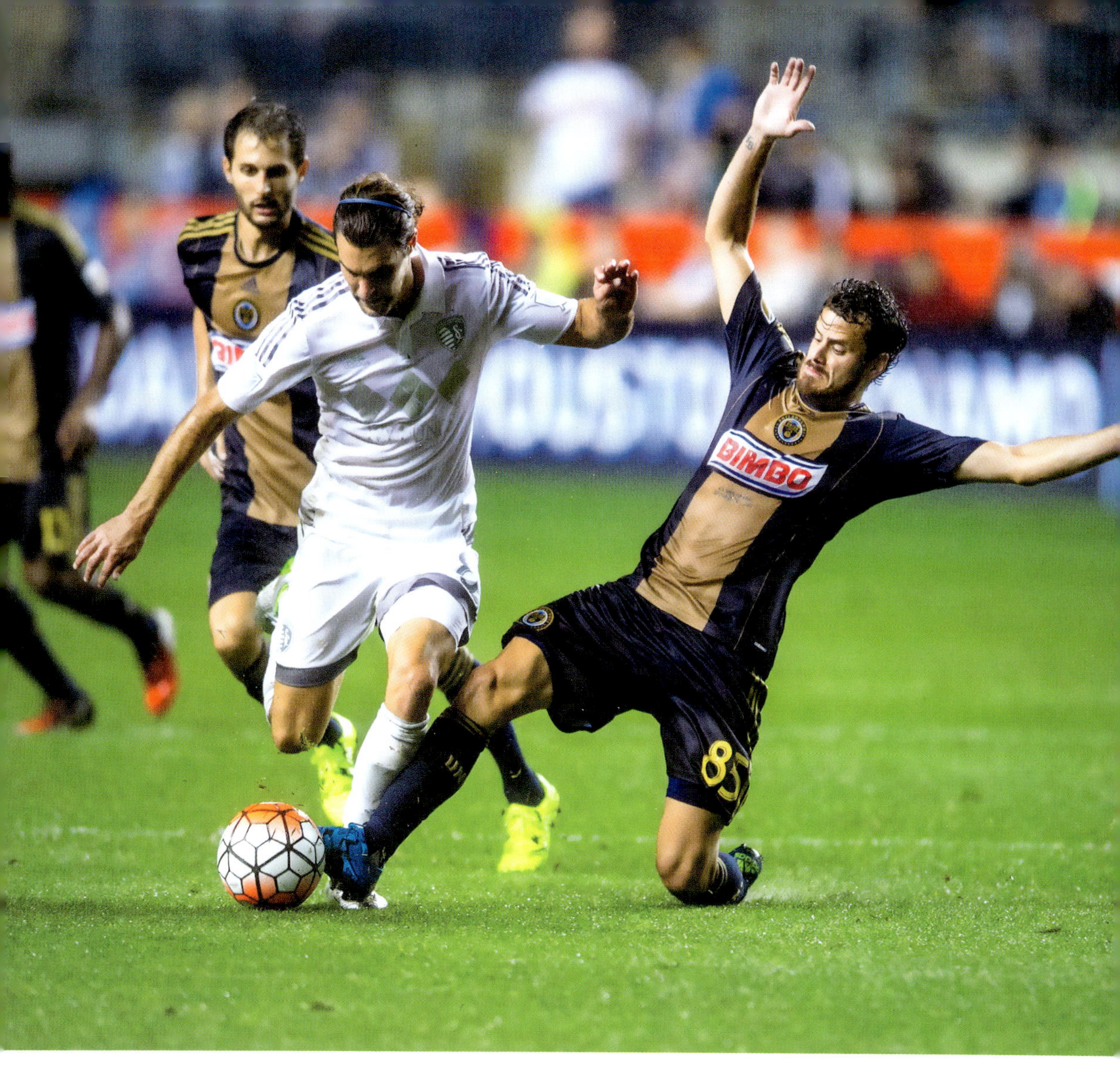

Tranquillo Barnetta, *right*, makes a sliding tackle against Graham Zusi of Sporting KC in the 2015 US Open Cup Final.

in 2016 after playing several years in Europe. An attacking midfielder by trade, Bedoya became the most expensive player in team history. His transfer from FC Nantes in France cost the Union $1 million.

Midfielder Alejandro Bedoya served as the Union's captain for much of his first four seasons in Philadelphia.

A member of the US national team from 2010 to 2017, Bedoya established himself as an anchor in the Union's midfield late in the 2016 season. He scored the opening goal in Philadelphia's first playoff win, a 4–3 defeat of the New York Red Bulls on October 20, 2019.

Defensive midfielder Brian Carroll's MLS career spanned from 2003 to 2017. The Fairfax, Virginia, native spent the final seven years of that career keeping opposing attackers in check with the Union. He had played more seasons with the Union than any other player at the time of his retirement in 2017.

ANCHORS IN THE NETS

Goalkeeper Andre Blake is one of the most beloved Union players of all time. The Jamaican had a standout college career with the University of Connecticut. Then Philadelphia selected him with the No. 1 overall pick of the 2014 MLS SuperDraft. Blake was a perfect pick for the Union, even though it took him a couple of seasons to earn the starting job.

Blake took over as the Union's top goalkeeper to start the 2016 season and made the most of it. He started 32 games that season after playing in just seven during his first two years with the team. He posted six shutouts and made 99 saves.

Andre Blake helped the Union earn back-to-back playoff appearances in 2018 and 2019.

He not only made his first MLS All-Star Game. He was named Goalkeeper of the Year.

Known for his ability to make incredible saves look routine, Blake had career highs with 118 saves and 10 shutouts in 2018. And two years after that in 2020, Blake won his second MLS Goalkeeper of the Year Award while leading the Union to their first Supporters' Shield as the league's best team in the regular season.

Blake brought stability to the goalkeeping position that had been lacking since Faryd Mondragón's one wonder year for the Union in 2011. The Colombian was 39 years old when he joined Philadelphia following a long international career. He provided leadership to the young team in front of him. His seven shutouts and 49 saves in 27 games helped lead Philadelphia to the playoffs in just its second year in the league.

ACADEMY SUCCESS

Some MLS teams rely on expensive transfers to build their rosters. The Union decided to go all in on their youth academy. That was already paying off by 2020. Midfielder Brenden Aaronson and defender Mark McKenzie became regulars for the Union. Both made their US national team debuts in December. By then, however, Aaronson was off to play in Europe. McKenzie would join him a month later. It was a success story for the Union's player development program.

CHAPTER 4

FINDING THEIR WAY

Among the biggest days in the history of the Union, April 10, 2010, stands out. The Union were still looking for their first victory after a 2–0 loss at Seattle in their MLS debut. With their new stadium yet to be completed, the Union moved to their temporary address at Lincoln Financial Field, the home of the Eagles. With the additional seating available at the football stadium, nearly 35,000 fans were on hand for the Union's first home opener.

The game marked the beginning of a new rivalry with nearby DC United. The granddaughter of US Vice President Joe Biden helped open the game by performing the ceremonial first kick. The Sons of Ben marched into the

Union players celebrate after Sébastien Le Toux completed his hat trick to beat DC United in the team's first home match.

stadium by the thousands. Once there, they sang and banged on drums to help carry the festive atmosphere.

Forward Sébastien Le Toux gave the Union a quick lead by scoring just four minutes into the game. He added another goal in the 40th minute to put the home team up 2–0 heading into halftime.

The Sons of Ben came out in force to support the Union in their home debut.

DC battled back to tie the game with two quick goals midway through the second half. The home fans wondered if they would have to settle for a draw. However, Le Toux played the part of the hero. He completed his hat trick in the 80th minute to put Philadelphia up for good at 3–2. Just over 10 minutes later, the final whistle blew, and the Union had the first win in team history.

COLONIAL CUP: A FRIENDLY RIVALRY

Philadelphia's victory was its first over DC United in a rivalry that has come to be known as the Colonial Cup. DC United initially called it "A rivalry for the people, by the people." A fan poll selected its official name in 2016.

The teams and cities have a special bond. Philadelphia was the original capital of the original 13 states. The hub of the government was later moved to nearby Washington, DC. In the 15 years before the Union existed, many Philadelphia soccer fans supported DC United, as it was the MLS franchise located closest to Philadelphia. The rivalry is one of the friendlier ones in the league due to the connection between the teams and the respect the fan bases have for one another.

TWO HOME OPENERS, TWO WINS

The Union completed a rare feat in 2010 by winning two home openers. They beat DC United in their first game in their temporary home. Then they opened their permanent home with a win as well.

On June 27, 2010, Philadelphia debuted its new soccer stadium in a match against the Seattle Sounders.

Union supporters packed the team's new stadium when it opened on June 27, 2010.

Now called Subaru Park, the stadium was originally named PPL Park. It was built on the waterfront in the Philadelphia suburb of Chester. Construction problems delayed the stadium's opening. However, the Union were scheduled to play eight of their first 10 games on the road. That meant they only had to play two games at Lincoln Financial Field before their new home was ready.

The stadium, built exclusively for soccer, provides a view of the Commodore Barry Bridge connecting Pennsylvania with

New Jersey. The bridge towers over the southwest corner of the stadium, giving some travelers a bird's-eye view of the game as they drive into or out of Chester.

A capacity crowd of 18,755 fans was treated to a 3–1 victory over the visiting Sounders on the Union's second Opening Day. But it didn't come easy. Seattle led 1–0 at halftime thanks to a goal by Pat Noonan. Le Toux again came to the rescue for United. First he tied it 10 minutes into the second half on a penalty kick. Later, Le Toux assisted on goals by Fred Carreiro and Danny Mwanga to give the Union a memorable victory.

PHILLY'S TOURNEY

The Union didn't have much success during their first decade. However, Philadelphia did advance to the final of the US Open Cup three times during its first 10 seasons.

Founded in 1914, the US Open Cup is a nearly year-long tournament open to all divisions of soccer in the United States. It is the oldest national competition in the country.

In 2014 the Union was in the middle of a four-year MLS playoff drought. But the club made it all the way to its first US Open Cup final that year. Philadelphia joined the tournament in the fourth round, when all MLS teams enter the competition. The Union won their first game over another team from Pennsylvania, the Harrisburg City Islanders of the lower-level United Soccer League.

Philadelphia then defeated the New York Cosmos, who played in another lower-division league that had adopted the old NASL name. Then the Union knocked off the New England Revolution of MLS to earn a spot in the semifinals.

The Union went on the road for the first time in the tournament to play at fellow MLS team FC Dallas. The score was tied 1–1 through regulation and extra time. That meant penalty kicks would determine a winner. Philadelphia won the shootout 4–3 to advance to the final. However, the Union were denied the first trophy in team history. Despite hosting the match, Philadelphia lost to Seattle 3–1 and had to settle for second place.

The Union reached the US Open Cup final again in 2015. But once

STARS UNITE

The Union's Carlos Valdés took the field at PPL Park on July 25, 2012. The defender wasn't playing for Philadelphia, though. He was a member of the MLS All-Star Team. They were playing English powerhouse Chelsea at the Union's home field. With a team featuring David Beckham, Thierry Henry, and Landon Donovan, the MLS All-Stars won 3–2 in front of a stadium-record 19,236 fans. Valdés checked in as a substitute late in the first half.

Philadelphia's Carlos Valdés is tripped up in the 2014 US Open Cup final against the Seattle Sounders.

again they lost on their home field, this time to Sporting Kansas City in a penalty kick shootout after the teams played to a 1–1 draw. Philadelphia made it back to the final again in 2018. For a third time, the Union were beaten in the championship game as host Houston claimed the trophy with a 3–0 win.

THE UNION RISE AGAIN

The Union didn't return to the playoffs until 2016. And in that trip they failed to win a game. But by 2019, the team's development efforts started to pay off.

Homegrown players such as midfielder Brenden Aaronson were playing key roles on the team. They were joined by international stars such as Kacper Przybylko of Germany, who led the team with 15 goals. The Union won a team-record 16 games to finish third in the conference and make the playoffs.

Expectations were high going into the playoffs. However, the visiting New York Red Bulls went up 3–1 at halftime. It looked like the same old story for the Union. Instead, in front of their raucous supporters, the Union staged an incredible comeback. Marco Fabián's goal in extra time secured a thrilling 4–3 victory. The Union had won their first playoff game.

The Union weren't able to advance any further. But in 2020, the club reached new heights. Przybylko again was a top scorer. Aaronson and fellow rising star Mark McKenzie played so well they earned moves to Europe after the season. Philadelphia posted the best record in all of MLS.

But familiar playoff woes came back. The Union lost to New England 2–0 in their first game. But with the world-class players it had developed, the team hoped it had finally built the foundation for a championship.

TIMELINE

2007	**2008**	**2009**	**2009**	**2010**
The Sons of Ben supporters group is founded.	MLS announces that Philadelphia has been granted an expansion team.	The team reveals its name and colors on May 11.	Piotr Nowak is introduced as the Union's first head coach on May 29.	The Union lose their first game 2–0 at Seattle on March 25.

2010	**2011**	**2014**	**2019**	**2020**
In their first home game on April 10, the Union pull out a 3–2 victory over DC United.	A 1–1 draw with Toronto FC on October 15 clinches the Union's first playoff berth.	Philadelphia loses to the Seattle Sounders in the US Open Cup Final on September 16.	The Union win a playoff game for the first time with a 4–3 victory over the New York Red Bulls on October 20.	Philadelphia posts the best record in MLS to win the Supporters' Shield for the first time.

TEAM FACTS

FIRST SEASON

2010

STADIUMS

Lincoln Financial Field (2010)
Subaru Park (2010–)

US OPEN CUP FINALS

2014, 2015, 2018

SUPPORTERS' SHIELDS

2020

KEY PLAYERS

Tranquillo Barnetta (2015–16)
Alejandro Bedoya (2016–)
Andre Blake (2014–)
Danny Califf (2010–12)
Sébastien Le Toux (2013–16)
Jack McInerney (2010–14)
Vincent Nogueira (2014–16)
Chris Pontius (2016–17)
C. J. Sapong (2015–18)

KEY COACHES

Jim Curtin (2014–)
John Hackworth (2012–14)
Piotr Nowak (2010–12)

MLS GOALKEEPER OF THE YEAR

Andre Blake (2016, 2020)

MLS COMEBACK PLAYER OF THE YEAR

Chris Pontius (2016)

MLS COACH OF THE YEAR

Jim Curtin (2020)

GLOSSARY

berth
A spot in a competition or tournament earned through previous result or results.

draw
A game that ends in a tie.

franchise
A sports organization, including the top-level team and all minor league affiliates.

hat trick
Three goals by a single player in one game.

homage
Special honor or respect shown publicly.

inaugural
The first, or marking the beginning of a significant event.

rival
An opponent with whom a player or team has a fierce and ongoing competition.

striker
Also called a forward, the player who plays nearest the opponent's goal.

wingback
A player who plays in a wide position on the field, taking part both in attack and defense.

MORE INFORMATION

BOOKS

Kortemeier, Todd. *Total Soccer*. Minneapolis, MN: Abdo Publishing, 2017.

Marthaler, Jon. *Ultimate Soccer Road Trip*. Minneapolis, MN: Abdo Publishing, 2019.

Trusdell, Brian. *Soccer Record Breakers*. Minneapolis, MN: Abdo Publishing, 2016.

ONLINE RESOURCES

To learn more about the Philadelphia Union, please visit **abdobooklinks.com** or scan this QR code. These links are routinely monitored and updated to provide the most current information available.

INDEX

ABOUT THE AUTHOR

Thomas Carothers has been a sportswriter for nearly 20 years in the Minneapolis–St. Paul, Minnesota, area. He has worked for a number of print and online publications, mostly focusing on prep sports coverage. He lives in Minneapolis with his wife and a houseful of dogs.